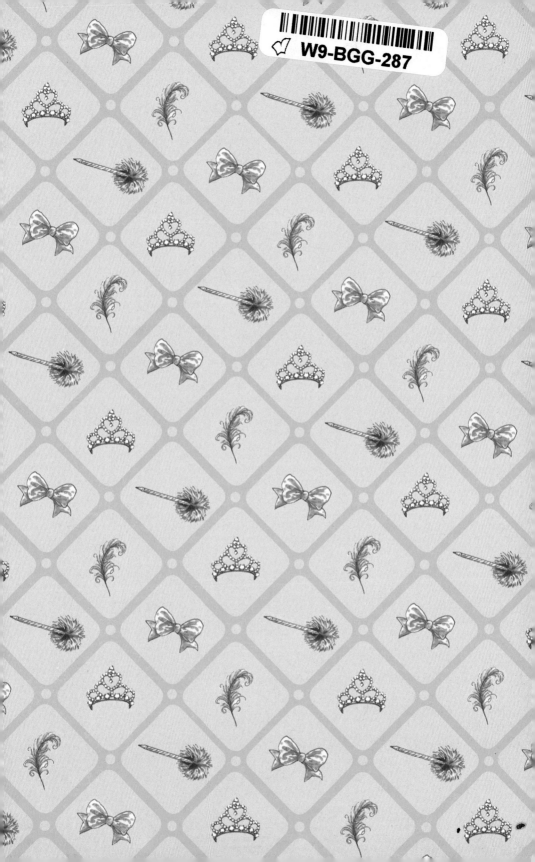

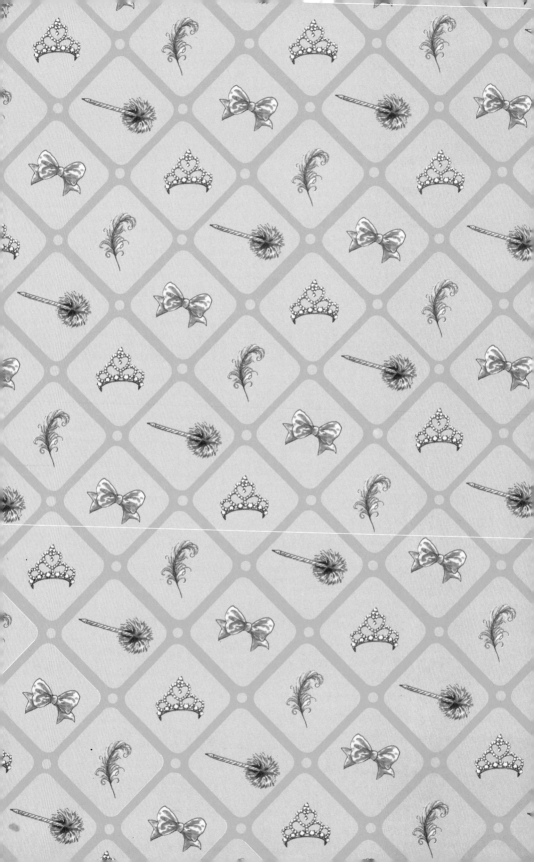

Dear Parent:
Your child's love of reading starts here!

Every child learns to read in a different way and at his or her own speed. Some go back and forth between reading levels and read favorite books again and again. Others read through each level in order. You can help your young reader improve and become more confident by encouraging his or her own interests and abilities. From books your child reads with you to the first books he or she reads alone, there are I Can Read Books for every stage of reading:

SHARED READING
Basic language, word repetition, and whimsical illustrations, ideal for sharing with your emergent reader

BEGINNING READING
Short sentences, familiar words, and simple concepts for children eager to read on their own

READING WITH HELP
Engaging stories, longer sentences, and language play for developing readers

READING ALONE
Complex plots, challenging vocabulary, and high-interest topics for the independent reader

I Can Read Books have introduced children to the joy of reading since 1957. Featuring award-winning authors and illustrators and a fabulous cast of beloved characters, I Can Read Books set the standard for beginning readers.

A lifetime of discovery begins with the magical words **"I Can Read!"**

Visit www.icanread.com for information
on enriching your child's reading experience.

1 BEGINNING READING

I Can Read!

Fancy NANCY

Treasury

by Jane O'Connor
pictures based on the art of
Robin Preiss Glasser

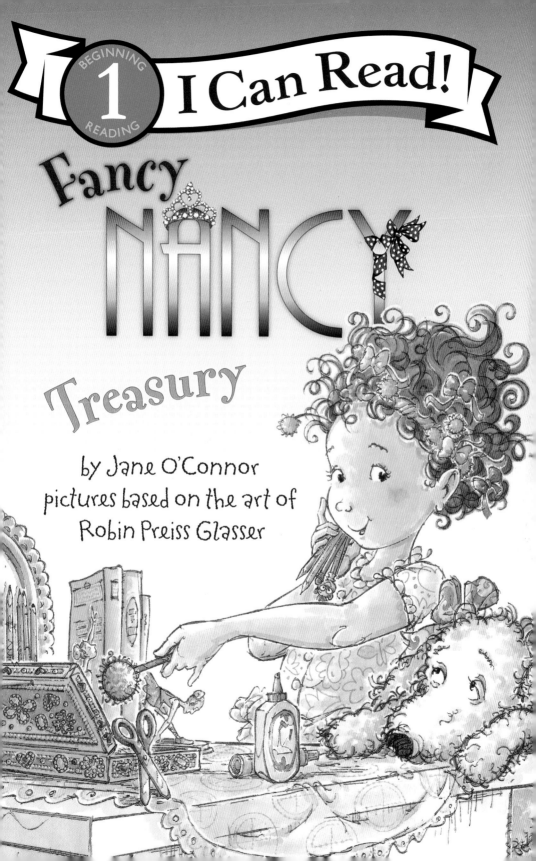

I Can Read!

BEGINNING 1 READING

Fancy NANCY Treasury

HARPER

An Imprint of HarperCollinsPublishers

Table of Contents

Fancy NANCY Pajama Day

by Jane O'Connor

cover illustration by Robin Preiss Glasser

interior pencils by Ted Enik

color by Carolyn Bracken

"Class, don't forget!"

Ms. Glass says.

"Tomorrow is . . ."

"Pajama Day!" we shout in unison.

(That's a fancy word

for all together.)

I plan to wear my new nightgown.

I must say, it is very elegant!

(Elegant is a fancy word

for fancy.)

Then the phone rings.

It is Bree.

She says, "I am going to wear

my pajamas with pink hearts

and polka dots.

Do you want to wear yours?

We can be twins!"

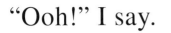

"Ooh!" I say.

"Being twins would be fun."

Then I look at my elegant nightgown.

What a dilemma!

(That's a fancy word for problem.)

Finally I make up my mind.

I tell Bree I am going to wear

my brand-new nightgown.

Bree understands.

She is my best friend.

She knows how much

I love being fancy.

The next morning at school,

we can't stop laughing.

Everyone's in pajamas,

even the principal.

He is carrying a teddy bear.

18

Ms. Glass has on a long nightshirt

and fuzzy slippers.

I am the only one

in a fancy nightgown.

That makes me unique!

(You say it like this: you-NEEK.)

"Nancy, look!" says Bree.

"Clara has on the same

pajamas as me."

Bree and Clara giggle.

"We're twins!" says Clara.

"And we didn't even plan it."

At story hour, Ms. Glass

has us spread out our blankets.

She reads a bedtime story.

Clara and Bree lie
next to each other.
"We're twins,"
Clara keeps saying.

At recess

Clara takes Bree's hand.

They run to the monkey bars.

"Come on, Nancy," Bree calls.

24

But it is hard to climb in
a long nightgown.
And I can't hang upside down.
Everyone would see
my underpants!

At lunch

I sit with Bree and Clara.

They both have grape rolls

in their lunch boxes.

"Isn't that funny, Nancy?"

asks Clara.

"We even have the same dessert."

I do not reply.

(That's a fancy word for answer.)

Pajama Day is not turning out

to be much fun.

I wanted to be fancy and unique.

Instead I feel excluded.

(That's fancy for left out.)

The afternoon is no better.

Clara and Bree are partners

in folk dancing.

Robert steps on my hem.

Some of the lace trim

on my nightgown rips.

At last the bell rings.

I am glad Pajama Day is over.

"Do you want to come
play at my house?"
I ask Bree.

But Bree can't come.

She's going to Clara's house!

I know it's immature.

(That's fancy for babyish.)

But I almost start to cry.

Then, as we are leaving,

Bree and Clara rush over.

"Nancy, can you come play too?"

Clara asks.

"Yes!" I say.

"I just have to go home first

to change."

Now we are triplets!

Fancy Nancy's Fancy Words

These are the fancy words in this book:

Dilemma—a problem

Elegant—fancy

Excluded—left out

Immature—babyish

Reply—answer

Unique—one of a kind (you say it like this: you-NEEK)

Unison—all together

Fancy NANCY

Peanut Butter and Jellyfish

by Jane O'Connor

cover illustration by Robin Preiss Glasser

interior illustrations by Ted Enik

Ooh la la!

Our class is at the aquarium.

We will see amazing creatures

that live in the sea.

First we have lunch in the cafeteria.

I open my lunch box.

Inside is a peanut butter

and jelly sandwich,

celery sticks with peanut butter,

and peanut butter cookies.

"The other day,

my dad made peanut butter,"

I tell Clara and Bree.

"He made way too much.

Pretty soon I am going to turn

into a peanut!"

Soon it is time to see the exhibits.

We see tropical fish

in every color you can imagine.

We watch sea otters playing
and see a dolphin show.
There is even a pool with manta rays
that we can touch.
(They feel like wet sandpaper!)

Then we come to a special exhibit.

The sign in front says,

"The Wonders of Jellyfish."

"I don't want to go in," I say.

"I detest jellyfish."

(Detest is fancy for hate.)

Once, at the ocean,

I got stung by a jellyfish.

"Don't look at them," Bree tells me.

"Just shut your eyes
and hold on to me."

Bree leads me through the exhibit.

Oops!

I bump into someone.

Oops again!

I bump into someone else.

Then I hear someone say,

"Nancy, is something the matter?"

I open my eyes partway.

It is Ms. Glass.

I explain why I detest jellyfish.

Ms. Glass says, "I understand.

I once got stung by a jellyfish.

But they are amazing sea creatures.

Come look."

Ms. Glass takes my hand.

I cup my hand over my eyes

so I only have to look a little.

50

We pass by a glass case
of big, blobby, brown jellyfish.
"Ew! Revolting!" I say.
(That means yucky and gross.)
But Ms. Glass keeps insisting that
jellyfish are amazing.

"Jellyfish don't have eyes or ears,"

Ms. Glass says.

"They don't have bones or a heart.

They are made mostly of water.

"The long strings are tentacles.

Those are what sting.

Often jellyfish sting

to defend themselves

against an enemy."

"I was not an enemy!" I tell her.

"I was just swimming

and having fun."

"Yes, but the jellyfish had no way of knowing that," Ms. Glass says.

"Jellyfish don't have brains, either."

I guess I see what Ms. Glass means.

The jellyfish wasn't out to get me.

It's not smart enough to do that.

We walk past a case of purple jellyfish.

They aren't as revolting

as the brown jellyfish.

Now we are standing in front of

lots of blue jellyfish.

You can see right through them.

(The fancy word for that

is transparent.)

Then we go stand by another case.

These jellyfish look like

pearly pink bubbles.

In the very last case are tons

of tiny jellyfish with lights.

They blink on and off like fireflies.

I am not so scared anymore.

I guess jellyfish are pretty amazing.

That night,

I tell my family about the aquarium

and the jellyfish.

"I am going to make a diorama

for Ms. Glass because she helped me

overcome my fear."

I explain to JoJo that

a diorama is a 3D display.

I get to work right after dinner.

I find an empty shoe box

and paint the inside blue.

Then I stick long, silvery ribbons

onto one of Mom's old shower caps.

I am making a jellyfish!

Dad helps me hang my jellyfish

from the top of the shoe box.

Then he clears the table.

(No one ate much dinner.

It was chicken

with peanut butter sauce.)

"Too bad I don't have sand

for the bottom," I say.

"Hold on," Dad tells me.

He gets out the giant jar

of homemade peanut butter.

We spoon the last of
the peanut butter
onto the bottom of the shoe box
until the jar is empty.
"It looks exactly like sand,"
I say.

Well, maybe not exactly,

but it's good enough.

I stick seashells

into the peanut butter sand.

Voilà! It looks spectacular.

(That's fancy for great.)

The next morning,

I present the shoe box

to Ms. Glass.

"Oh! A jellyfish diorama!"

she exclaims.

66

Then I giggle and say,

"No, Ms. Glass.

It's a peanut butter

and jellyfish diorama!"

Fancy Nancy's Fancy Words

These are the fancy words in this book:

Detest—hate

Diorama—a 3D display

Revolting—yucky and gross

Spectacular—great

Transparent—see-through

Fancy NANCY
Super Secret Surprise Party

by Jane O'Connor

cover illustration by Robin Preiss Glasser

interior illustrations by Ted Enik

Ooh la la!

Our class is throwing a party.

I can't reveal who it's for.

(Reveal is a fancy word for tell.)

I don't want to spoil the surprise.

"Everybody is on a committee.

A committee is a group

with a job to do,"

I tell my family at dinner.

"My committee is in charge
of refreshments."
Then I explain to my sister
that refreshments means food.

"Who is the party for?"

JoJo wants to know.

JoJo is not trustworthy.

She can't keep secrets.

So I say, "I am sorry.

I cannot tell you."

Then I lock my lips and throw

away the key.

The next day

our committee meets at recess.

Lionel will take care of beverages.

That's fancy for stuff to drink.

"I will bake cupcakes," I say.

Clara says,

"I'll bring chips

and popcorn for the party."

Uh-oh!

Grace overhears us.

That means she is listening in.

"Party? What party?"

she says really loudly.

Grace is not in our class.

She doesn't know about our party.

"*Shhhh.* It's a secret," I say.

"It's a surprise," says Lionel.

"You better invite me,"

Grace says.

Lionel shakes his head.

"Sorry. You can't come."

Right away

Grace starts yelling.

"That's mean!

I'm telling."

She points to Ms. Glass

and the other teachers.

Oh no!

She can't tell them.

It would be a disaster!

It would ruin everything.

We explain why the party is

just for our class.

"You have to keep it hush-hush,"

I say.

"You can't tell a soul."

Grace promises.

But Grace is not always trustworthy.

We make her lock her lips

and throw away the key.

After school,

Annie takes us shopping.

She is a teenager

and babysits for us sometimes.

Bree is on the decorating committee.
Decorating means making
our classroom look fancy.
She buys balloons and streamers.

We run into Robert.

He is on the supplies committee.

He is buying

paper plates and napkins.

"Who is the party for?" Annie asks.

Annie is very trustworthy.

So we confide in her.

(Confide is like reveal.

It's another fancy word for tell.)

Still we make Annie lock her lips

and throw away the key.

In the supermarket,

I buy a box of cupcake mix.

It is called Chocolate Surprise.

That is perfect

for a surprise party!

That night

Dad and I bake the cupcakes.

Then we frost them.

They are chocolate with

tiny marshmallows inside.

The marshmallows are the surprise.

The next morning

everyone in our class

comes to school very early.

We decorate the room.

Yoko has made a giant card.

All it needs is our signatures.

Signature is fancy for writing out

your name.

So? Have you guessed

who the surprise party is for?

Yes! It's for Ms. Glass!

She walks in

and we all shout, "Surprise!

Happy birthday!"

Ms. Glass is so surprised,
she can't say a word.
She is speechless.

We give Ms. Glass the card.

We sing "Happy Birthday."

Then we have juice and cupcakes.

Mmmmm. The cupcakes are delectable.

That's fancy for yummy.

"So how old are you, Ms. Glass?"

Lionel wants to know.

Ms. Glass smiles.

"That's a secret," she says.

Then she locks her lips

and throws away the key.

Fancy Nancy's Fancy Words

These are the fancy words in this book:

Beverages—drinks

Committee—a group with a job to do

Confide—tell

Decorating—making something look fancy

Delectable—yummy

Overhears—listens in

Refreshments—food

Reveal—that means tell, too

Signature—writing out your name

Trustworthy—able to keep secrets

Fancy NANCY

It's Backward Day!

by Jane O'Connor

cover illustration by Robin Preiss Glasser

interior illustrations by Ted Enik

Today all the kids walk
into school like this.

"Good-bye," we say to Ms. Glass.

"Good-bye," Ms. Glass says to us.

Then we all sit down.

Nobody faces Ms. Glass.

Why is everything topsy-turvy?

(That's fancy for

upside down and super silly.)

It's Backward Day!

Look what the kids are wearing.

Lionel has on sunglasses
and a tie.

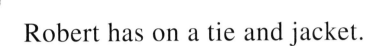

Robert has on a tie and jacket.

Clara's hair is in a French braid.

Ooh la la!

It looks fancy and backward.

Bree and I have on purple hoodies.

We wear socks on our hands.

So does Ms. Glass.

She also wears a tutu for a hat.

I adore my topsy-turvy teacher.

First we all say the alphabet.

We have to start with *z, y, x*.

"This is easy," Lionel says.

He means that it's hard!

Next Ms. Glass reads us a story.

She starts on the last page!

"I don't like Backward Day

at all," Lionel says.

He means he likes it a lot.

Then we make name tags.

Here are our backward names.

They are nonsensical.

That is also fancy for super silly.

At lunch we eat dessert first.

Lionel has cookies.

Ooh la la!

They look delectable.

That is fancy for yummy.

113

"I won't share with you,"

Lionel says.

"That's not nice," I say.

Then Lionel shouts,

"Ha-ha! I'm joking.

It's Backward Day.

I'm saying that

I WILL share my cookies."

He gives me two!

In the yard

we divide into teams

for races.

We have to run backward.

It is extremely hard.

Extremely is fancy for very.

117

"I'm sorry we're
on the same team,"
Lionel says to me.

I start to get mad.

But Lionel is joking again.

He really means that he's glad

we're on the same team.

It's Backward Day!

Later Ms. Glass says,

"What shall we do next?

I have no more backward ideas."

I look around the room
at all the topsy-turvy outfits.
Ooh la la! I have an idea.
"Let's have a fashion show—
a backward fashion show."

Lionel makes a face.

So do some other boys.

"No!" he says.

"Fashion shows are no fun."

This time Lionel is not joking.

"Ha-ha!" I shout.

"This time YOU forgot.

It's Backward Day.

You just said that

fashion shows ARE fun."

Lionel knows I got him this time.

We all model our ensembles.

Ensemble is fancy for clothes.

After the fashion show,

it's time to go home.

"Hello," we say to Ms. Glass.

"See you yesterday."

And that is the beginning—

I mean the end—

of this story.

Fancy Nancy's Fancy Words

These are the fancy words in this book:

Delectable—yummy

Ensemble—clothes

Extremely—very

Nonsensical—super silly

Topsy-turvy—upside down and super silly

Fancy NANCY Best Reading Buddies

by Jane O'Connor

cover illustration by Robin Preiss Glasser

interior illustrations by Ted Enik

Ooh la la!

I am so fortunate.

That's fancy for lucky.

I have a reading buddy.

On Mondays we read together.

Violet is in fifth grade

and very mature.

That means she acts grown-up.

She wears cool clothes.

"I don't like to match," she says.

"I like to look original.

That means different."

Violet shows me her feet.

Even her shoes don't match!

That night

I try on lots of clothes.

"I don't like to match,"

I tell JoJo.

"I like to look original."

Then I try reading to JoJo.

But she wants to play instead.

She is not a good reading buddy.

Not like Violet.

Violet and I like
all the same books.
Isn't that fortunate?

Sometimes I read to Violet.

I sound out the hard words.

"You are a great reader,"

she tells me.

"*Merci*," I say.

"That's French for thanks!"

Later we go to the cafeteria.

We eat and chat.

Violet wants to be

a librarian someday.

Me too!

Today Violet reads a funny book
about a girl and her little sister.
The little sister gets into mischief.
Mischief is fancy for trouble.

"She is like my little sister!"

I say.

"Mine too," Violet says.

Violet shows me a picture

of her sister.

At home,

I take a picture of JoJo

from the album.

I want to show it to Violet

next Monday.

But next Monday

I wake up with a cold.

I have to miss school.

I do not get to see Violet.

It hurts my eyes to read.

So my dad reads to me.

He chats with me too.

My dad is very kind.

But I miss my reading buddy.

The Monday after that,

Violet's class has a trip.

So we can't read together.

She waves from the school bus.

144

"That's my reading buddy,"

I tell Lionel.

Lionel and I sit on a low bar
on the jungle gym.
The high bars make us dizzy.
"I miss my reading buddy.
I won't see her till next Monday."

Lionel shakes his head.

"There's no school Monday.

It's a holiday. Lucky us!"

But I don't think

that is fortunate at all.

Monday comes.

At breakfast my mom asks,

"Why do you look sad?"

I start to explain about missing

my reading buddy.

But then the phone rings.

My mom answers it.

A minute later

my mom says,

"Quick! Quick! Get dressed."

Before I can ask why,

she scoots me upstairs.

I am tying my shoes
when the doorbell rings.
"Nancy, go answer it,"
my mom calls to me.

151

I open the door and there is . . .

Violet!

"I miss reading together,"

Violet says.

"So my mom called your mom.

You're spending the day with us.

Guess where we are going first!"

We are going to the library,
of course.
We pick out lots of books
to take home.

I get a book

about a girl from Paris.

Violet finds another book

about the naughty little sister.

After that

we go for ice cream.

We sit in a booth in the back.

Violet and I split

a banana split.

Then I read my book to her.

She helps me with the hard words.

I am so fortunate.

I have the best reading buddy

in the world.

Fancy Nancy's Fancy Words

These are the fancy words in this book:

Fortunate—lucky

Mature—acting grown-up

Merci—French for thanks

Mischief—trouble

Original—different

Fancy NANCY
Time for Puppy School

by Jane O'Connor

cover illustration by Robin Preiss Glasser

interior illustrations by Ted Enik

I am thrilled.

Thrilled means excited—only
fancier.

School starts soon.

I will miss Frenchy very much.

All summer

we played together.

I simply adore Frenchy.

Adore means love, love, love.

Frenchy is the best dog ever.

But sometimes she is naughty.

That means she gets into trouble.

Frenchy watches me

plan my ensemble for school.

Ensemble is fancy for outfit.

Frenchy wants to play

tug-of-war with my belt.

"No," I tell her.

"Belts are not toys."

Now I need to find my backpack.

Here it is!

It looks too small for me.

I grew a lot this summer.

I show my backpack to Mom.

Mom says, "We can buy a new one."

Then she runs into the kitchen.

"No," she tells Frenchy.

"You can't jump up on the table!"

The next day,

my mom and I go shopping.

I pick out a purple backpack.

At home

I tie ribbons around the straps

and make big bows.

I write out my name in jewel stickers.

Voilà!

In French that means "Look at that!"

Now my new backpack is perfect.

At dinner

I tell my parents,

"I am going to learn so much at school.

By the end of the year,

I may even be a genius."

(A genius is a super-smart person.)

I have to talk very loudly.

That's because Frenchy is barking.

She wants some of our dinner.

"No barking," my dad tells her.

"This is people food—not dog food."

After dinner I run upstairs
to get my new backpack.
I want to show my mom and dad
how fancy I made it.

Oh no!

Somebody pulled off the fancy stuff.

And I know who did it!

Frenchy!

"Frenchy, that was very naughty!"

I say.

Frenchy looks so sorry.

I give her a big kiss.

I really do adore her.

My mom hears me talking to Frenchy.

She sees what Frenchy did.

"You know what?

I think Frenchy needs to go

to puppy school!" she says.

Puppy school! Ooh la la!

Frenchy starts on Monday.

I let her wear my old backpack.

It is filled with puppy treats.

All the dogs are adorable.

That's fancy for cute.

We watch the teacher train the dogs.

Frenchy learns a lot.

By the end of the week,

Frenchy plays with only her toys.

She does not bark and beg for food.

Even at home

Frenchy leaves people stuff alone.

She really is the best puppy ever.

The night before school,

I get out my ensemble.

I put new ribbons

and stickers on my backpack.

Then I give Frenchy a kiss

and tickle her tummy.

"You were a very good student!

I am proud of you."

It's funny.

Frenchy is all done with school.

And I haven't even started yet!

Fancy Nancy's Fancy Words

These are the fancy words in this book:

Adorable—cute

Adore—love, love, love

Ensemble—outfit

Genius—super-smart person

Naughty—gets into trouble

Thrilled—excited

Voilà—look at that